Mitford
at the
HOLLYWOOD
ZOO

by Donald Robertson

story by Drue Robertson

VIKING

Mitford, the tallest fashion assistant *ever*, was happy to be going to the best *job* ever. Every day Mitford zoomed uptown on a BlueCity Bike . . .

bought a latte from Tar Ducks,

and then took the elevator up, up, up, to the offices of *Cover* magazine.

One morning, Mitford had just taken a sip of a delicious Tar Ducks latte, when Panda Summers, the editor-in-chief of *Cover* magazine and Mitford's boss, threw open her office door.

"It's a fashion disaster!" she screeched, dropping her latest Poochie Panda bag.

Rhinoana, the off-the-charts celebrity singer and *Cover* magazine's cover model for the upcoming Hollywood issue, was doing a photo shoot in L.A. before her performance at the Academy Zoowards. But she had just spilled Zoom Juice all down the front of her one-of-a-kind haute couture cotton-candy dress, and it had *disintegrated*. Now she had *nothing* to wear!

Sniff, sniff, sniffed Mitford.

"Exactly!" sniffed Panda. She took off her super-silly inside sunglasses and squinted at Mitford. "You're good at fixing things, Mitford. We'll send you to L.A. If you can find a perfect dress for Rhinoana *and* get some fabulous photos for the Hollywood issue, then I will promote you to fashion editor at *Cover* magazine!"

And before Mitford could sniff again, a flight was
booked, bags were packed, and Mitford was on the way
to Jaguardia Airport!

After landing in L.A., Mitford hailed a limo and they slowly—thanks
to traffic—crawled their way to the Sunset Bow-Wow Hotel, where
Rhinoana was staying.

The photographer Annie Labovitz was sipping a Bow-Wow Barktini by the pool. "She's in there," she grumbled, pointing at a cabana. "And if she won't come out in five minutes, I have other animals to shoot."

"None of these clothes fit me right!" Rhinoana whined, nibbling on her purple polished nails.

Sniff, sniff! Mitford immediately understood. Nothing fit giraffes right either.

A butterfly flew in the window. All of a sudden, Mitford got an idea. Mitford ran to the hotel's concierge desk and explained what was needed. *Tout de suite!*

Within minutes, dozens of containers of Zoom Juice had arrived. Mitford poured every one on Rhinoana.

"Ooooooh," she squealed, as more butterflies flew through the window and landed on her.

"Butterflies *love* Zoom Juice," explained Mitford.

"*BEE-YOOTIFUL!*" cooed Rhinoana.

"Simply *stunning*!" said Annie Labovitz,
from behind her camera.

"I can't thank you enough!" cried Rhinoana, hugging Mitford—
very carefully. "You *must* come to the Academy Zoowards.
I'll be singing. Just wear something fabulous!"

Panda surprised Mitford in the lobby.

"I decided to go to the Zoowards, after all," she sniffed.

"My friend the stylist Iris Apefeld is swamped and could use your help."

"Mitford!" cried Iris. "Just the giraffe I was looking for!"

The Zooward-winning actress Meryl Sheep had just arrived in Iris's costume shop. She was looking a bit bedraggled from her latest film.

"She can't go to the Zoowards looking like *that*," whispered Iris. "What can we do??"

Something in Iris's shop gave Mitford an idea.

A somewhere-over-the-raindow idea!

Mitford grabbed an electric razor and all of
Iris's dyes and paints and went to work.

Iris Apefeld went *bananas*! "This is amazing!" she exclaimed.
"Now Meryl Sheep is sure to stand out on the red carpet!"

But the giraffe couldn't stay in Iris's studio for long. Mitford's phone was ringing again, and it was the celebrity stylist Rae H. L. Zooey at her shop in Venison Beach.

"I've got a *huge* Fashion Emergency!" Rae H. L. yelped, before the sound of waves drowned her out.

Sniff, sniff! went Mitford, and calmly looked up Metro directions for Venison Beach.

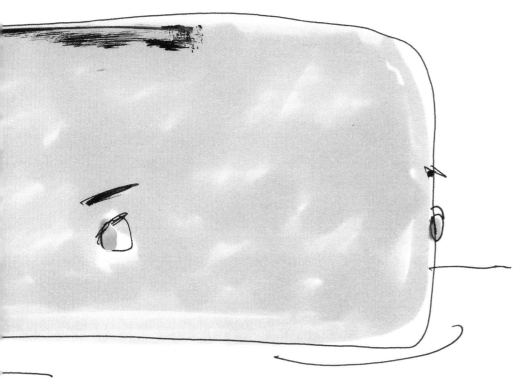

Kiss, kiss, went Mitford, arriving at Rae H. L. Zooey's super chic shop.

"See!" said Rae H. L.

"He *is* huge," agreed Mitford, staring at Shark Whaleberg.

"And he's nominated for a Zooward, but it's black tie only!"

Mitford squinted into Rae H. L.'s big black mascaraed eyes. "How much waterproof mascara do you have?"

Rae H. L. didn't have that much mascara, but she did have plenty of waterproof surfboard paint! Soon Shark Whaleberg was covered from tip to tail.

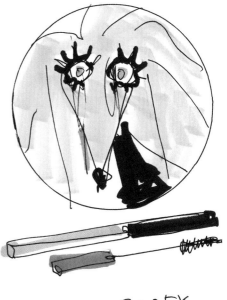

RAE H. L. ZOOEY LOVED SPIDER LASH WATERPROOF MASCARA. (BEAUTY CREDIT)

Ring, ring! Panda was calling from her hair appointment with Serge Bearmont.

"Did you find something to wear, Mitford? I need you to interview everyone on the red carpet! Pick me up in half an hour!"

TREND ALERT!

Rae H. L. grabbed a paint roller, and the giraffe
stood very still.

"Don't get paint on the bus seats!" she called as
Mitford galloped away.

Twenty minutes later, Mitford picked up Panda at the hotel and escorted her to the red carpet at the Zoowards. Everyone who was anyone in Hollywood was there, including Brad Pitbull, Angelina Collie, and Bee Yonsay.

"I *love love love* your new hairstyle!" exclaimed Ryan Seahorse to Panda Summers. "And, who's your gorgeous date?"

Flashbulbs flashed. Mitford posed.

Panda presented Rhinoana with the awards for Best Song *and*
Best Costume Design.
Meryl Sheep won for Best Hairstyling.
Shark Whaleberg won for Best Actor in a Marine Role.
And Mitford won a promotion—to Fashion Editor
of *Cover* magazine!
Sniff, sniff.

"Congratulations!" said all of Mitford's new Hollywood friends.
Kiss, kiss!

Dedicated to Bill Cunningham
and all the "fashion kook–loving" gentle giants.
You will be missed. *Sniff, sniff!*

VIKING
An imprint of Penguin Random House LLC
375 Hudson Street
New York, New York 10014

First published in the United States of America by Viking, an imprint of Penguin Random House LLC, 2017

LIBRARY OF CONGRESS CATALOGING-IN-PUBLICATION DATA IS AVAILABLE
ISBN 9780451475435

Manufactured in China

1   3   5   7   9   10   8   6   4   2

Set in Century Expanded

The art for this book was rendered on paper using paint, markers, tape, and black pen.